I0456532

Tamacun

David Robertson

Published by Tomorrow's Tales, 2024.

TAMACUN

First edition. June 24, 2024.

ISBN: 979-8991025911

Written by David Robertson.

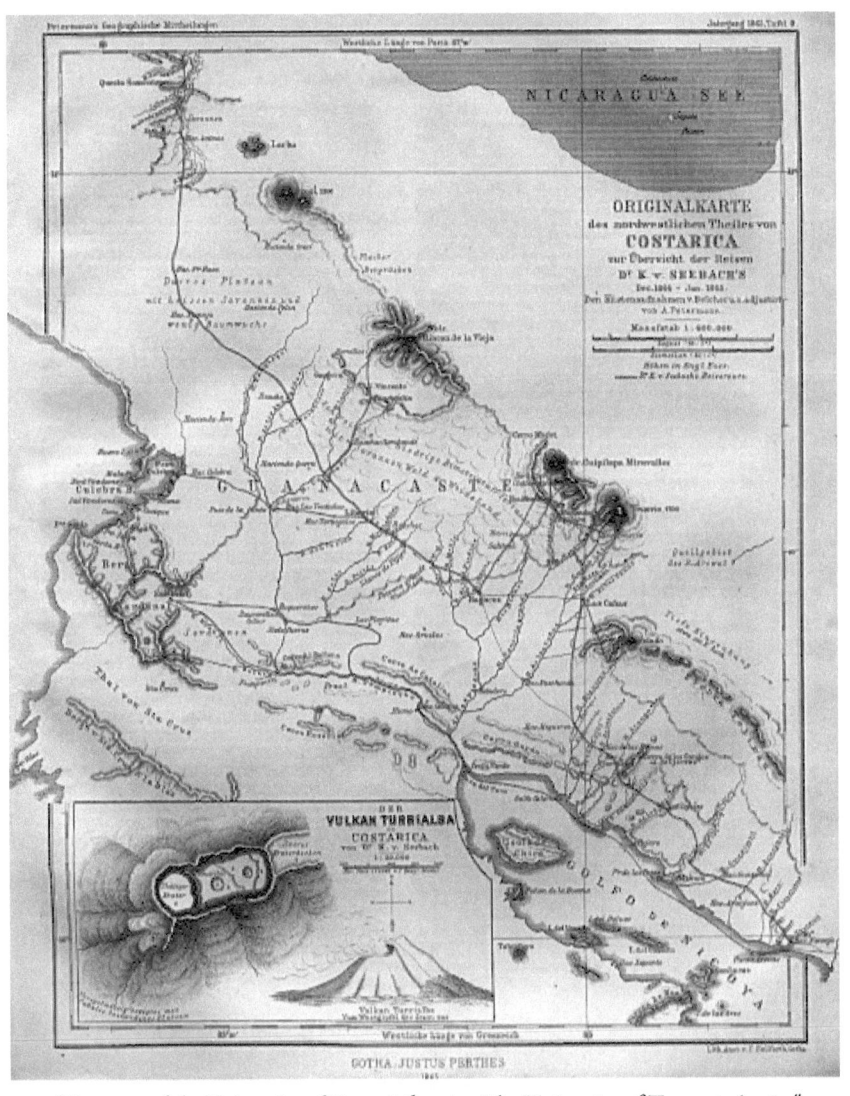

"Courtesy of the University of Texas Libraries, The University of Texas at Austin."

Arrival

EVERYTHING WAS DIFFERENT here. Being from Germany, Karl Albert Ludwig von Seebach was no longer surrounded by the comforts of home. The salt of the sea spray coming in from the Caribbean Ocean had a distinct smell. In fact, every seaport in a foreign land had its own distinct smell. He had been to many places around the world documenting volcanic activity and its geology, so while there was much here that was different from the others, it was all strangely familiar at the same time. Puerto Limón was a big city in this part of the world. Travelers came and went as did materials imported to support some level of civilization. Raw goods left for kingdoms and empires thousands of miles away. It had taken Karl more than seven weeks since his departure from Hamburg to get this far, after a brief change of ship in Havana.

"Well," started Carl August Bolle who was traveling with him, "I believe we have found the place." It was a bit out of place for him to still speak his native German in this foreign land, but for them it was innate. Karl had met Carl at an ornithological conference a few years ago. Karl was here for the fire and sulfur; Carl was here for the birds.

The bustling port of Puerto Limón was alive with activity, a symphony of sounds that spoke of distant lands and endless possibilities. Dockworkers shouted instructions as they unloaded crates of bananas, coffee, and exotic hardwoods, while merchants haggled over prices with sailors who had crossed the vast Atlantic. Karl inhaled deeply, savoring the mingling scents of saltwater, ripe fruit, and the earthy undertones of the rainforest beyond.

Karl made his way through the crowded streets, his senses overwhelmed by the vibrant colors and unfamiliar aromas. Stalls lined the narrow alleys, each offering a cornucopia of local delicacies. He paused at one such stall, drawn by the enticing scent of sizzling meat. The vendor, a stout woman with a warm smile, offered him a skewer of grilled pork marinated in a blend of spices that hinted at the tropics.

"Try this, señor," she said in heavily accented Spanish. "It's called 'chicharrón'. Muy delicioso."

Karl accepted the offering, biting into the succulent meat. The flavors exploded in his mouth—smoky, sweet, and just a hint of heat from the local peppers. He nodded appreciatively to the vendor, who beamed at his reaction.

Further along, he encountered a stall piled high with vibrant fruits he had never seen before. He picked up a bright orange orb, its surface dimpled and slightly rough.

"Maracuyá," the vendor explained, seeing Karl's curiosity. "Passion fruit. Very good for the energy."

Karl purchased a few, the vendor expertly slicing one open to reveal the fragrant, jelly-like seeds inside. He scooped out a spoonful, savoring the tart sweetness that danced on his tongue. The exotic fruit was a far cry from the apples and pears of his homeland, a reminder of the new world he had stepped into. Carl, spoke no words, but held up a hand, unwilling to venture into the exotic just yet.

With his hunger sated, Karl continued his exploration of the city. The architecture of Puerto Limón was a blend of colonial influences and local flair. Brightly painted wooden houses with ornate balconies lined the streets, their facades weathered by the salty air. The people were equally diverse, a tapestry of cultures and ethnicities that reflected the city's history as a melting pot of immigrants, indigenous peoples, and Afro-Caribbean communities.

As he wandered, Karl's mind was already turning to the task ahead. The Rincón de la Vieja volcano, known locally as Tamacún, awaited him. The stories he had heard spoke of its temperamental nature—eruptions, fumaroles, and boiling mud pots. It was a geological wonder, and Karl was determined to uncover its secrets.

Finding a guide in this foreign land was essential. Karl had heard tales of the treacherous jungle that lay between Puerto Limón and the volcano, a dense tangle of vegetation teeming with wildlife, both benign and deadly. He needed someone who knew the land intimately, who could navigate the labyrinth of trails and keep them safe from the myriad dangers that lurked within.

Karl made his way to a modest inn recommended by one of the sailors on his ship. The innkeeper, a wiry man with a weathered face, greeted him warmly.

"Buenos días, señor. How can I help you?"

"I need a guide," Karl replied, switching to his rusty Spanish. "Someone who can take us to Rincón de la Vieja." He gestured to Carl who had followed him in and was inspecting the room as his colleague inquired.

The innkeeper's eyebrows rose. "Tamacún? That's a dangerous journey. But I know just the man for you. His name is Manuel. He's a local, knows the jungle like the back of his hand."

Karl nodded, relief washing over him. "Can you arrange a meeting?"

"Of course. He usually comes by in the evenings. Why don't you settle in and rest? I'll send for him."

Karl thanked the innkeeper and both men retired to their room, the exhaustion of the long voyage finally catching up with him. He lay on the bed, his mind drifting to the adventures that awaited him in the heart of Costa Rica. The thought of the volcano, with its fiery heart and untamed power, filled him with a mixture of excitement and trepidation.

The other Carl neatly packed his things into a provided armoire, and then began to wash his face and prep for a light shave. "Just how long are you staying," the other inquired.

"There is nothing like a fresh shave after a long journey," his companion stated as he continued his business. "This might be the last good one I get for many days. Let's find a good dinner, for the same reason."

Karl rolled his eyes and then closed them. This man he had chosen for this trip might wind up more trouble than he is worth, but at least he had some familiar company. It was not uncommon for a team of guides to lead foreigners into the jungle, only to hold them hostage or threaten to leave unless some extortion payment was made. But surely this would not be one of those expeditions.

As evening fell, Karl made his way to the inn's common room. The air was thick with the scent of tobacco and the sound of lively conversation. He spotted the innkeeper, who gestured for him to join a table where a rugged-looking man sat nursing a cup of coffee.

"Señor von Seebach, this is Manuel."

Manuel looked up, his dark eyes assessing Karl with a sharp intelligence. He extended a calloused hand. "Pleasure to meet you. So, you want to see Tamacún?"

Karl shook his hand firmly. "Yes. I need a guide and a team to help me get there. I've heard it's a dangerous journey. This is Carl, who will be joining us," he said gesturing towards his colleague, who had followed him into the room.

A bit perplexed, Manuel stated, "Karl y Carl? Esta bien, señores." He then nodded as he continued. "It is a dangerous journey. The jungle is unforgiving, and the volcano is unpredictable. But I can take you there. We will need supplies, and I will gather a few men I trust."

"How soon can we leave?" Karl asked, eager to begin the expedition.

"Give me two days to prepare," Manuel replied. "We must be well-equipped for this journey."

Karl agreed, feeling a surge of anticipation. Manuel returned the next day and introduced the Germans to the rest of the team: Juan, a burly man with a talent for setting up campsites; Miguel, a young but experienced tracker; and Luis, who knew the medicinal plants of the jungle and could treat injuries and ailments.

The Destination: Tamacún (Rincón de la Vieja) Volcano

THE EASY PART WAS FORMING a team for the excursion west. Arguably, the harder part was finding supplies in a limited market and then determining how they would get them to their destination. Manuel was skilled in these matters and went around the city looking for the right people. Juan was with him, but Karl stayed behind to draft a plan to get to Tamacún without it taking longer than his journey by sea to get here. Soon Manual would return and he could fill in the gaps with his extensive knowledge of the forests that lay between them and their target.

Karl sat at a weathered wooden table in the dimly lit room of their temporary lodgings, the flickering candlelight casting shadows on the walls. He spread out a map of Costa Rica before him, tracing his finger along the winding paths and dense jungles that separated them from their destination. Tamacún, or Rincón de la Vieja as it was also known, loomed in the distance like a sleeping giant, its peak obscured by mist and mystery.

Carl August Bolle, his native companion on this daring journey, had proven to be a valuable asset. Their shared passion for exploration had forged a bond that now propelled them into the heart of the unknown. Karl could only hope that their combined expertise would be enough to navigate the treacherous terrain that lay ahead.

As Karl sketched out their route, Manuel burst through the door, a grin spreading across his weather-beaten face. "I've found us a guide," he announced triumphantly, his voice echoing off the walls. "An old friend of mine who knows these forests like the back of his hand."

Karl nodded in approval, relief washing over him. With Manuel's connections and their guide's expertise, their chances of success had just increased tenfold. But there was still much to be done before they could set out on their journey.

"First, we need to purchase supplies," Karl said, folding up the map and tucking it into his satchel. "We'll need enough provisions to last us for the duration of the trip, as well as equipment for navigating the jungle safely."

With Manuel leading the way, they set out into the bustling streets of Puerto Limón, weaving their way through the throngs of people and stalls selling exotic fruits and spices. It was a chaotic scene, but Manuel seemed to know exactly where to find what they needed.

After several hours of haggling and bargaining, they finally emerged from the marketplace laden with small sacks of rice, dried meats, and other essential provisions. Given their limited carrying capacity, some things would be harvested along the way. Water would not be a problem in this part of the world, but purifying it was essential to avoid any unnecessary misadventures. Karl breathed a sigh of relief as they made their way back to their lodgings, their arms full and their pockets considerably lighter.

Back at the inn, they set about packing their supplies into sturdy canvas sacks, making sure to distribute the weight evenly for ease of carrying. It was a tedious task, but one that was necessary for their journey into the unknown.

"Bad news, señores," Luis mentioned as he walked into their room. The others were just finishing up.

"Que pasó?" inquired Manuel.

Luis continued with a look of disappointment over his face. "My cousin cannot make it. He is very sick and cannot make the journey."

"Luis' cousin is also our guide," clarified Juan as he continued to pack supplies.

"We have no guide?" exclaimed Carl, obviously concerned.

Karl, however, was confident in the men who were present and said as much. "Manuel has always been our guide. Luis, I am sorry that your cousin cannot travel with us, but so be it. We will be fine. We leave in the morning. Do not be late."

With their supplies secured and their plan in place, Karl felt a sense of anticipation building within him. Tomorrow, they would embark on their journey to Tamacún, where adventure and danger awaited them at every turn. But for now, they would rest and prepare for the challenges that lay ahead.

As the sun dipped below the horizon and the sounds of the city faded into the distance, Karl found himself filled with a sense of excitement unlike any he had ever known. For he knew that their journey was only just beginning, and that the greatest adventures were yet to come.

• • • •

On the morning of their departure, Karl stood at the edge of the city, looking out at the dense wall of greenery that marked the beginning of their journey. Manuel clapped him on the shoulder.

"Ready, señor?" Manuel asked. Scurrying about next to him was some odd-looking animal. His loyal companion, a coatimundi named Chico, was an endearing presence throughout their expedition. Chico, with his sleek, rust-colored fur and bushy, ringed tail, had an inquisitive nature that mirrored Manuel's own adventurous spirit. His long, flexible snout and sharp claws made him adept at foraging for food, often seen rummaging through the underbrush for fruits and insects. Despite his wild origins, Chico was remarkably affectionate, frequently curling up beside Manuel during their nightly campfires and chittering softly as if sharing in the human camaraderie. His playful antics, from climbing trees with ease to teasing the other members of the team, provided a much-needed source of amusement and comfort in the heart of the unforgiving jungle. The bond between Manuel and Chico was evident in the way the coati followed his master faithfully.

Carl was the first to speak, his face unsure of this creature or its purpose in their party. "What is this thing? Surely, he is not necessary."

"Señor," retorted Juan, "do not underestimate Chico. He has saved the lives of many men on similar journeys. He might save yours too." Carl simply stood there looking at the animal, perplexed by the entire exchange.

Karl took a deep breath, feeling the weight of his equipment and the thrill of the unknown. "Ready."

With that, they plunged into the jungle, the sounds of Puerto Limón fading behind them. The adventure had begun.

• • • •

As they ventured deeper into the rainforest, the canopy closed overhead, filtering the sunlight into a dappled mosaic on the forest floor. The air grew thick with humidity, and the calls of exotic birds echoed through the trees. Karl marveled at the vibrant ecosystem around him, each step revealing new wonders and challenges.

The first few days of travel were grueling. The terrain was uneven, and the dense undergrowth made progress slow. Manuel and his team moved with practiced ease, their machetes slicing through the foliage. Karl struggled to keep up, his legs aching from the constant exertion. But he pressed on, driven by the promise of discovery.

However, Carl was not as committed to this path. "Are there no roads? No rivers of transit?" He had only researched the birds that lived in the jungles but had neglected to make inquiries as to what the infrastructure was like to get to them. Sure, it was jungle, but how much of it?

"Roads, señor?" Luis added and then followed with a wink of the eye, "Only if you build them." All of the guides erupted with laughter. Even Karl smiled at the thought.

Costa Rica was a young country and far away of most of the busier trade routes. It lacked the natural resources other places had, making it undesirable for modern investment, especially given the dense jungle that seemed to swallow everything soon after they had left Puerto Limón. Anything like a road or a rail line was merely wishes for the men who led them into the unknown.

One evening, as they set up camp by a crystal-clear stream, Manuel approached Karl with a serious expression.

"We need to be cautious," he said. "The jungle is alive with dangers—jaguars, snakes, and even the spirits of the forest."

Karl raised an eyebrow. "Spirits?"

Manuel nodded. "The locals believe in the spirits of the jungle. They say the forest is protected by ancient guardians. I've heard stories of strange occurrences, people disappearing without a trace."

Karl felt a shiver run down his spine but dismissed it as superstition. He had faced many dangers in his career, and he was not about to let ghost stories deter him.

That night, as he lay in his hammock, the sounds of the jungle enveloped him. The rustling of leaves, the distant howl of a monkey, and the chirping of insects created a symphony that lulled him to sleep. But his dreams were filled with images of the volcano, its fiery heart calling to him.

Leaving Civilization Behind

IT WAS SLOW GOING, something the two German men were not accustomed to, especially Carl. Being a specialist in birds, he had travelled to many places, but those were often coastal areas to places near great rivers that could be traversed with ease by boat. Even the mountains of Germany and Austria—where his family was from—were easier to pass through than this. It was all vegetation, all the time. Their guides worked constantly and diligently, but the jungle was unforgiving and also unwilling to give up its secrets or its content easily. Up a hill and down the other side, it was a lot of work just to make it a several miles each day, it seemed. How long was it to the volcano? he thought.

Karl sympathized with his friend's plight. Though he had more experience with volcanic regions, the dense rainforest posed its own set of challenges. Each step seemed to resist, the jungle vines and roots threatening to trip them at every turn. The air was thick with humidity, clinging to their clothes and making every breath feel like a laborious effort.

As they trudged forward, the constant buzz of mosquitoes filled the air, their incessant bites an ever-present torment. Manuel had provided them with a local repellent, a mixture of herbs and oils, but even that seemed to offer little respite. Karl swatted at the pests, feeling a fresh sting on his neck despite his best efforts to keep covered.

"These infernal insects," Carl muttered, slapping his arm. "I thought I knew what discomfort was, but this is something else entirely."

Manuel, ever the patient guide, turned back to them with a sympathetic smile. "The jungle tests all who enter, my friends. But we are making good progress. Just keep your spirits high and your eyes open."

The terrain grew more challenging as they pressed on, the undergrowth thicker and the path steeper. Each ascent was a test of endurance, their legs burning with the effort. The afternoon rains added another layer of difficulty, turning the path into a muddy quagmire that sucked at their boots and slowed their pace even further.

Karl and Carl struggled to keep their footing, often relying on the sturdy roots of trees to pull themselves up the slippery slopes. The rain, relentless and heavy, drenched them to the bone. There was no escaping its reach, and soon they were all soaked, their clothes clinging uncomfortably to their skin.

"How much further, Manuel?" Carl asked during one particularly arduous climb, his voice strained with effort.

"Not far now," Manuel replied, though Karl suspected he said it more for encouragement than accuracy. "The rain will pass, and we will find a good spot to rest."

True to Manuel's word, the rain eventually subsided, leaving behind a steaming, mist-laden jungle. They continued their march, their spirits buoyed by the sight of a clear sky overhead. The sun, though not yet visible, began to filter through the canopy, casting a warm, golden glow on the rainforest floor.

As the day wore on, the heat became oppressive, the jungle turning into a stifling furnace. The combination of humidity and high temperatures sapped their strength, making every step a Herculean effort. Karl felt his shirt sticking to his back, the sweat pouring off him in rivulets.

"Is it always this hot?" Carl asked, his face flushed and dripping with sweat.

Manuel chuckled. "This is the jungle, señor. It is alive with life and heat. Today is the mostly heat."

They paused frequently to drink water and rest, seeking out the shade of large trees to escape the worst of the sun's rays. Chico, ever the curious coati, scampered about the campsite, his antics a welcome distraction from the exhausting conditions. He darted up trees and sniffed at their packs, his bright eyes full of mischief.

Despite the heat and the fatigue, Karl marveled at the resilience of their guide and his team. Manuel, Juan, Miguel, and Luis moved with a quiet efficiency, their familiarity with the jungle evident in their every action. They set up camp swiftly, gathered firewood, and prepared meals with practiced ease, their movements almost instinctual.

One evening, as they sat around the campfire, Luis shared stories of the jungle's many wonders. He spoke of plants that could heal wounds and others that were deadly if touched. His knowledge was vast, a testament to his deep connection with the land.

"Do you believe in the spirits of the jungle, Luis?" Karl asked, recalling Manuel's earlier warnings.

Luis nodded solemnly. "The jungle is full of mysteries, señor. There are things we cannot see but we can feel. It is wise to respect them."

Karl pondered this as he lay in his hammock that night, the sounds of the jungle lulling him to sleep. The journey was pushing them to their limits, but it was also revealing the profound beauty and complexity of the natural world.

· · · ·

The next morning, they continued their trek, the path becoming increasingly rugged as they neared the foothills of some volcano. The dense forest gave way to a more open landscape, the trees sparser and the ground rockier. The change in scenery was a welcome relief, offering a clearer path forward.

As they moved through a narrow gorge, the sound of a distant roar stopped them in their tracks. Karl's heart raced as he scanned the surroundings, his eyes trying to pierce the shadows cast by the towering cliffs on either side.

"What was that?" Carl whispered, his voice trembling.

Manuel held up a hand for silence, his eyes narrowing as he listened intently. The roar came again, closer this time, a low, guttural sound that sent chills down their spines.

"Jaguar," Manuel said quietly, his hand moving to the machete at his belt. "We must be cautious. They are territorial and can be very dangerous."

The group huddled together, their eyes darting nervously around the rocky terrain. Suddenly, a flash of movement caught Karl's eye. A sleek, spotted form emerged from the shadows, its yellow eyes locking onto them with predatory intent.

The jaguar moved with a fluid grace, its muscles rippling beneath its glossy coat. It stalked towards them, its powerful body low to the ground, ready to pounce. Karl's breath caught in his throat as he realized the danger they were in.

Before anyone could react, Chico sprang into action. The fearless coatimundi darted forward, placing himself between the jaguar and the group. He hissed and chattered aggressively, his fur bristling as he tried to make himself appear larger.

The jaguar paused, seemingly taken aback by Chico's audacity. It snarled, baring its teeth, but the coati held his ground, his sharp claws and teeth at the ready.

In a blur of motion, the jaguar lunged at Chico, its powerful jaws snapping shut just inches from the brave animal. But Chico was quick, dodging to the side and swiping at the jaguar's face with his claws. The jaguar roared in frustration, its eyes blazing with fury.

Manuel seized the moment, his machete flashing in the sunlight as he stepped forward to protect his beloved pet. Juan and Miguel joined him, their own weapons at the ready, while Luis and Karl kept Carl safely behind them.

For a tense moment, it seemed as though the jaguar might attack again. But Chico's relentless bravery, combined with the formidable presence of the armed men, was enough to deter the great cat. With a final growl, the jaguar turned and slunk back into the shadows, disappearing as swiftly as it had appeared.

The group let out a collective sigh of relief, their bodies trembling with the adrenaline of the encounter. Manuel knelt down and scooped Chico into his arms, his face a mixture of pride and relief.

"Gracias, Chico," he murmured, stroking the coati's fur. "You saved us."

Chico chirped in response, nuzzling into Manuel's chest. The bond between them was clear, a testament to the deep connection that had formed over years of companionship.

"I told you, señor," said Juan to both German men, giving Carl a smile. "We do not die today." And with that he walked off to grab his gear and continue on.

As the sun began to set, casting a warm glow over the rugged landscape, they found a suitable spot to set up camp for the night. The stream nearby provided fresh water, and the sound of its gentle babbling offered a soothing backdrop to their evening preparations.

Karl sat by the fire, his mind replaying the events of the day. The jungle was a place of unparalleled beauty and danger, a world where the line between life and death was often blurred. But it was also a place of wonder, where the spirit of adventure thrived and the bonds of friendship were tested and strengthened.

As they settled into their hammocks, the sounds of the jungle once again lulling them to sleep, Karl felt a renewed sense of purpose. The journey to Rincón de la Vieja was far from over, and there were undoubtedly more challenges ahead. But with companions like Manuel, Carl, and even the fearless Chico by his side, he was ready to face whatever the jungle had in store.

The adventure had truly begun, and Karl knew that the secrets of Tamacún were within reach. All they had to do was keep moving forward, one step at a time, through the heart of the untamed wilderness.

Encountering The Natives

PEOPLE HAVE LIVED HERE long before the Spanish arrived. The jungle was alive which made it a place that attracted people, flora and fauna. It wasn't the easiest place to thrive but is was easy enough to survive. Water was everywhere in some form and with the daily rains, it was easy enough to clear some of the vegetation to grow some agriculture. The soil was not good enough to provide for a large harvest, but things would grow here. Everything seemed to grow, in fact. The Spanish quickly determine that when fence posts were placed to contain the animals they brought with them, it did not take long before the very fence posts began to regrow themselves.

Karl and Carl marveled at these stories Manuel shared as they trekked deeper into the jungle. Each day brought new challenges and new discoveries. The sheer density of the forest, its myriad of sounds, and the pervasive sense of being watched weighed heavily on their minds. They felt like intruders in a place where every leaf and shadow had a history unknown to them.

One humid afternoon, as they descended into a lush valley, the group was caught unawares. Out of the dense underbrush, figures emerged, blending almost seamlessly with the foliage. They were surrounded by indigenous warriors, their faces painted with intricate patterns, their eyes sharp and wary.

The sudden appearance of these warriors stunned Karl and his companions. Manuel tried to speak, raising his hands in a gesture of peace, but the warriors moved swiftly, disarming them and binding their hands with surprising gentleness yet unyielding firmness. Chico hissed and chattered, but a soothing murmur from Manuel calmed the coatimundi.

"We mean no harm," Manuel said in the local dialect, his voice steady despite the tension. "We are travelers, explorers seeking knowledge, not conquerors."

The leader of the warriors, a tall man with a feathered headdress, regarded Manuel with a discerning gaze. After a moment, he nodded, gesturing for the group to follow. They were led through a series of twisting paths, the jungle seeming to swallow them whole as they moved deeper into the unknown.

Karl's mind raced as they walked. The prospect of meeting indigenous people had always fascinated him, but this sudden capture was beyond anything he had imagined. He glanced at Carl, whose face was a mix of fear and curiosity. Both men knew that their fate now lay in the hands of these jungle inhabitants.

They arrived at a clearing where a village lay hidden beneath the thick canopy. Simple huts constructed of wood and thatch dotted the landscape, smoke rising from cooking fires. The villagers watched them with a mixture of suspicion and interest as they were brought before the tribe's elders.

The elders sat in a semicircle, their expressions unreadable. Manuel stepped forward, bowing respectfully before speaking in their language. He explained their purpose, detailing the scientific nature of their journey and their respect for the land and its people. The elders listened in silence, their eyes shifting between the captives and Manuel.

After what felt like an eternity, the leader of the elders spoke. His voice was calm but commanding, and though Karl did not understand the words, he could sense the gravity of the situation. Manuel translated, explaining that the tribe was wary of outsiders due to past encounters with hostile invaders.

"They fear we bring danger," Manuel said, looking at Karl and Carl. "But they are willing to listen. We must show them we mean no harm and can offer something in return."

Luis stepped forward, producing a small pouch from his bag. He knelt before the elders, carefully laying out various herbs and plants. He spoke of their medicinal properties, demonstrating his knowledge and respect for the jungle's gifts. The elders murmured among themselves, clearly impressed by Luis's expertise.

Next, Juan demonstrated his skills with setting up a camp, showing the efficiency and care with which they treated their temporary homes. Miguel showcased his tracking abilities, explaining how he could help them navigate and protect the tribe's territory.

Finally, Karl and Carl offered their knowledge of the natural world. Carl described the birds they had encountered, drawing sketches of the species unique to this part of the jungle. Karl spoke of the volcanic activity, explaining their mission to understand the earth's secrets, not exploit them.

The elders conferred quietly, the tension in the air palpable. After a lengthy discussion, the leader stood and addressed them. Manuel translated with a relieved smile.

"They will allow us to stay, but we must prove our intentions through our actions. We are to be watched, but we are not prisoners."

Karl felt a wave of relief wash over him. They had been given a chance to continue their journey, albeit under close scrutiny. The tribe's acceptance was tentative, but it was a start.

As night fell, the group settled into the village, their guards ever watchful but less tense. Karl and Carl marveled at the resilience and resourcefulness of the villagers, their way of life deeply connected to the rhythm of the jungle. Chico, sensing the shift in atmosphere, explored the village with curious enthusiasm, endearing himself to the children who giggled at his antics.

Just as they began to feel a sense of uneasy peace, a sudden commotion erupted at the edge of the village. Shouts and cries filled the air as a rival group of warriors launched a surprise attack. The village was thrown into chaos, the air thick with the sounds of conflict.

The native tribes of Central America led lives of resilience and resourcefulness, intricately connected to the lush, unforgiving environment of the region. Their existence was one of constant adaptation and vigilance, shaped by both the bounty and the perils of the jungle.

Life in the jungle was fraught with danger, not only from the natural world but also from rival tribes. Conflict was an ever-present threat, and the ability to defend their territory was essential for survival. The warriors of the tribe were highly skilled in the art of jungle warfare, their knowledge of the terrain giving them a significant advantage.

Before a battle, the warriors would paint their bodies with intricate designs using dyes made from plants and minerals. These markings were not only for intimidation but also held spiritual significance, believed to protect the wearer and imbue them with the strength of their ancestors. Armed with bows, arrows, spears, and machetes, they moved through the jungle with silent precision, their every step a testament to years of training and tradition. The warriors who had now attacked this village were indeed covered in paint meant to intimidate their prey.

Ambushes were a common tactic, utilizing the dense foliage to conceal their movements. The element of surprise was their greatest ally, and the ability to strike swiftly and disappear into the jungle was a skill honed to perfection. The jungle was a master of disguise, its thick growth and myriad of plants concealing the dangers that lay beyond sight. On this night, the jungle was their enemy, and not a friend.

Karl and his companions found themselves caught in the midst of the melee. Despite their bonds with the tribe, they were still seen as outsiders, and the attackers showed no hesitation in targeting them. Manuel, Juan, Miguel, and Luis fought valiantly alongside the villagers, their skills and courage making a significant impact.

In the fray, Karl saw a flash of movement—a jaguar, its eyes gleaming with a predatory light. But this was no wild beast; it was a symbol of the attacking tribe, its presence a harbinger of danger. Before Karl could react, the jaguar lunged toward him, its powerful form a blur of fur. But this was no ordinary jaguar; rather, a warrior wearing the pelt of one, his face marked with a menacing appearance of the jaguar's own face. He was armed with a knife with which he would use in close combat.

Chico, sensing the imminent threat, sprang into action once more. The coatimundi darted forward, his sharp claws and teeth a whirlwind of defiance. He leaped onto the jaguar, distracting it long enough for Karl to scramble to his feet. Manuel and Juan rushed to his aid, the latter wound up facing this half man, half jaguar.

The two came together and locked arms, neither able to gain the advantage. Both men were abnormally strong which caused them to stalemate for several minutes; each received cuts and bruises from knife and fist. The fighting had taken them from the open village into the jungle, perhaps by the jaguar's design. Surprise was a jaguar's primary weapon and the vegetation here made for clumsy fighting. It was difficult to see ahead three feet, much less one's opponent.

As the jaguar lept towards him from beyond a low bush with thick branches, Juan dropped his knife and reached for a vine that hung next to his body. Its beginnings started somewhere out of sight in the canopy above. Next, when the jaguar was close, he grabbed it with one hand while wrapping the vine around the jaguar's neck with the other. Stopping cold in his tracks, the jaguar writhed back and forth, securing itself to the vine. Now it was completely tangled which limited its movement. Juan took that moment to stoop down, grab his knife and put an end to the jaguar. He would harm no one else this night.

The battle raged on, the village a chaotic battleground. The rival warriors fought fiercely, but the defenders, bolstered by their new allies, held their ground. The attackers, realizing they could not overcome the combined forces, began to retreat, melting back into the jungle's shadows.

As the dust settled, the villagers regrouped, tending to the wounded and assessing the damage. The tribe's leader approached Karl and his companions, his expression one of gratitude and respect.

"You have proven yourselves," Manuel translated, his voice filled with pride. "You fought alongside us, and for that, we are in your debt."

Karl nodded, feeling a deep sense of camaraderie with the villagers. They had faced a common enemy and emerged stronger for it. As they helped rebuild and tend to the injured, Karl knew that their journey was far from over. The jungle held many more secrets and dangers, but they were no longer strangers in this land.

The tribe leader spoke once again which Manuel translated, "He says we must go to Arenal."

"What is Arenal?" asked Carl.

"Arenal is a place, señor, a volcano," replied their guide. "I have been there once and can take us there."

• • • •

As night fell once more, they found a place to rest near a stream, the soothing sound of water a balm to their weary spirits. Chico curled up beside Manuel, his small body a reminder of the courage that could be found in even the smallest of creatures.

Karl lay back, gazing up at the stars that peeked through the canopy. The journey to Tamacún was a path fraught with peril and wonder, but with his companions by his side, he felt ready to face whatever lay ahead. The adventure had only just begun, and the heart of the jungle still called to them with its mysteries and promises. And now they had a new adventure. This Arenal was an added bonus, provided more calamities did not find them before they got there.

Detour to Arenal Volcano

IT DID NOT TAKE LONG for them to land upon the foothills of the Arenal Volcano, even while navigating the jungle. One benefit of these majestic and mighty survivors of time is that they cleared a lot of jungle often enough that it could not overtake them. That left lots of open spaces around them, and in more extreme cases, scarred landscapes miles from their summit.

Arenal itself was one of the most beautiful things Karl had ever seen. It stood tall and could be seen many miles away. Mottled greens and browns dotted it from the foothills to the summit, with great variegation in between. Some trees familiar to them from the jungle wandered up and down its slopes, but those were very sparse and scattered in small groups of three or seven. It was obvious there was a battle going on between Arenal and the jungle that surrounded it.

The volcano was a towering giant, standing at approximately 1,670 meters (5,479 feet) above sea level, its conical shape rising majestically against the backdrop of the sky. The lush, verdant vegetation at its base gave way to sparser, hardier plants as the elevation increased, a testament to the harsh conditions closer to the summit. The air was cooler here, carrying a crispness that contrasted sharply with the dense, humid jungle below.

Despite its serene beauty, Arenal was a sleeping giant, a volcano known for its periodic displays of power. Historical records and local legends spoke of its eruptions, the most notable being in 1801-03. Although not much detailed information was available from that time, it was known that these eruptions had reshaped the landscape, depositing layers of ash and volcanic rock that could still be seen. The memory of these past events lingered in the minds of those who lived near its shadow, a constant reminder of the potential danger.

The flora around Arenal was a mix of resilient species that had adapted to the volcanic soil. The nutrient-rich earth, replenished by occasional ash deposits, supported a unique ecosystem. Orchids, bromeliads, and ferns thrived, their vibrant colors standing out against the darker volcanic rock. Birds and small mammals, drawn by the abundant plant life, flitted and scampered through the underbrush, adding life to the otherwise stark landscape.

The journey up Arenal's slopes was both challenging and awe-inspiring. Trails wound through dense patches of forest, where the canopy was so thick that sunlight barely penetrated. In other areas, the path opened up, offering breathtaking vistas of the surrounding countryside. The ground underfoot varied from soft, loamy soil to rough, uneven terrain, a mix of hardened lava flows and loose volcanic ash.

Karl could not help but marvel at the resilience of life here. The battle between the jungle and the volcano was evident in the way plants clung tenaciously to every available surface, roots winding through cracks in the rocks, leaves reaching for sunlight. It was a place of stark contrasts, where life and destruction coexisted in a delicate balance.

The local people, too, had a deep respect for Arenal. They spoke of it in hushed tones, referring to it as both a giver and a taker. The fertile soil around its base provided for their crops, but the threat of an eruption was a constant presence. They had stories of ancestors who had witnessed the volcano's wrath, tales passed down through generations as both warnings and reminders of the natural world's power.

As they continued their ascent, Karl and his companions could feel the weight of history and nature pressing in on them. The beauty of Arenal was undeniable, but so too was the danger it represented. It was a place where the earth's raw power was laid bare, a testament to the dynamic forces that shaped the land.

In the quiet moments, as they paused to catch their breath or take in the view, Karl felt a profound connection to this land. It was a feeling of being part of something much larger, a small cog in the vast, ever-turning wheel of nature.

Karl and his companions—Carl, Manuel, Juan, Miguel, and Luis—stood in awe of the sight. The dense jungle canopy had given way to a more open landscape, allowing them a clear view of the volcano. The air was different here, carrying with it a slight tang of sulfur, a reminder of the power lying dormant beneath the earth.

They set up camp at the base of the volcano, the warm glow of their fire contrasting against the darkening sky. As night fell, they marveled at the stars, which seemed brighter and more numerous than they had ever seen. The beauty of the moment was a stark contrast to the treacherous path that had brought them here.

Morning broke with an uneasy calm. They began their ascent, navigating the uneven terrain with caution. Karl, ever the meticulous observer, noted the changes in the landscape as they climbed higher. Vegetation became sparse, replaced by rocks and ash, remnants of past eruptions. And as they neared the summit, the sense of awe and reverence only grew stronger, the knowledge that they were standing on the edge of a powerful, living monument to the earth's enduring spirit.

Without warning, the ground trembled beneath their feet. The air filled with a low, ominous rumble that grew louder with each passing second. Panic spread through the group as they realized the volcano was waking.

"Luis, look out!" Manuel shouted, but it was too late. A torrent of molten rock and ash burst forth from the volcano's mouth, cascading down its slopes with terrifying speed. Luis, caught in the path of the eruption, had no time to react. He was struck by a large fiery rock that had been blasted out of the side of Arenal, his anguished cries swallowed by the roar of the eruption. When they got to him, he was already dead.

The group was thrown into chaos. Karl and Carl struggled to maintain their footing, their faces pale with fear and shock. Manuel, tears streaming down his face, instructed Juan to grab Luis. They had to leave quickly; the rocks were still falling around them and small landslides were happening to either side of them.

"Retreat! We must retreat!" Juan bellowed, his voice cutting through the din. They scrambled down the slope, the heat of the eruption searing their skin. They didn't stop until they reached a safer distance, breathless and grief-stricken.

· · · ·

The eruption had subsided by the time they reached the base, but its aftermath was devastating. The landscape was scarred, ash blanketing the ground where lush vegetation once thrived. Their friend and companion, Luis, was gone.

In solemn silence, they gathered what remained of their belongings. Manuel, his face etched with sorrow, led them to a small clearing where they would bury Luis. They worked with heavy hearts, digging a grave with their hands and makeshift tools.

Karl spoke a few words, his voice choked with emotion. "Luis was more than a guide. He was a friend, a brother in this journey. His knowledge and spirit will remain with us as we continue."

They placed a simple marker on the grave, a testament to Luis's life and sacrifice. The jungle around them was eerily quiet, as if mourning the loss of one of its own.

Exhausted and emotionally drained, the group continued their journey. Manuel led them to a place he had been on his previous visit here, a place of healing and respite. The hot springs of Tabacón, nestled in the heart of the jungle, promised a brief respite from their grief and fatigue.

The springs were a natural wonder, steaming pools of mineral-rich water heated by the volcanic activity beneath the earth. As they approached, the soothing warmth and gentle steam enveloped them, a stark contrast to the harrowing ordeal they had just endured.

They disrobed and entered the water, the heat seeping into their aching muscles. For the first time in days, they allowed themselves to relax, the tension and sorrow slowly ebbing away. Chico, the ever-faithful coatimundi, scampered around the edge of the pools, his presence a comforting reminder of the jungle's vibrant life.

Carl sighed, leaning back against a smooth rock. "We have lost much, but we must remember why we are here. Luis's sacrifice will not be in vain."

Manuel nodded, his eyes closed as he soaked in the warm water. "We will honor him by continuing our journey. The volcanoes, the jungle—they are not just obstacles, but part of the story we are meant to tell."

As night fell, the hot springs glowed softly under the light of the moon. The group found solace in each other's company, their bond strengthened by the trials they had faced. They knew the journey ahead would be fraught with danger and uncertainty, but in this moment of peace, they found the resolve to continue.

Karl gazed up at the stars, his thoughts turning to the adventures yet to come. The memory of Luis would travel with them, a silent guardian watching over their path. And as they drifted off to sleep, cradled by the warmth of the springs, they dreamed of the journey to Tamacún and the secrets it held.

The Birds of Guanacaste

THE NEXT MORNING WAS hazy, the skies hosting various colors of gray with mottled blues. Arenal was silent but looming in the distance. Perhaps today it would awaken, or some other day, but it would be soon. The ground still shook periodically with small tremors and everyone in the party was eager to get away from here. They would say their goodbyes to both Arenal and Luis.

Partly to distract them from volcanoes and the dangers they had just faced, Manuel suggested they continue through the Guanacaste region west of Arenal and approach Tamacún from the south. This would also take them through a major birding area which very much excited Carl. To this point, he had journalled several bird species and their habits, but it was more of an afterthought as so much of their time required them to focus on traveling from one camp to another.

With their path decided, they gathered their belongings and set off. The terrain gradually changed as they moved westward, the dense jungle giving way to a more open forest. The air was fresher, less humid, and the sunlight filtered through the canopy, casting dappled shadows on the forest floor. It was a welcome change, and Carl could hardly contain his excitement as he spotted birds flitting through the trees.

The Guanacaste region was a birder's paradise, teeming with avian life. The calls of parrots and toucans filled the air, their vibrant plumage adding splashes of color to the green landscape. Carl moved with a newfound energy, his eyes constantly scanning the treetops and underbrush. He pointed out species to Karl, Manuel, and the rest of the team, sharing his knowledge with infectious enthusiasm.

"Look there, a resplendent quetzal," Carl whispered, pointing to a flash of emerald and crimson in the trees. "And over there, a keel-billed toucan! Such a marvelous beak!"

Karl smiled at his friend's excitement. It was good to see Carl in his element, his earlier weariness forgotten. Even Manuel, Juan, and Miguel seemed more at ease, the tension of their recent ordeal with Arenal easing as they walked through this tranquil forest.

Their journey through Guanacaste was not without its challenges, though. The terrain was still rugged, and they had to navigate through rivers and over rocky hills. Mosquitoes were a constant nuisance, and the afternoon rains turned the paths into slippery, muddy tracks. But the abundance of birdlife kept their spirits high, and Carl's joy was contagious.

One afternoon, as they were resting by a clear stream, they heard a strange, unearthly cry from above. The sound was unlike any birdcall they had heard before. Carl looked up, his eyes widening in astonishment.

"What in the world...?" he began, but his voice trailed off as he saw the source of the noise.

Above them, soaring on leathery wings, were creatures that seemed to belong to a different era. Pterosaurs, with their long, pointed beaks and bat-like wings, circled high above the canopy. The sight was both awe-inspiring and terrifying.

"Are those...?" Karl started, but Manuel interrupted.

"Pterosaurs," Manuel confirmed, his voice low. "Ancient creatures, rarely seen. We are indeed in a place of wonders and dangers."

The group watched in silent amazement as the pterosaurs glided overhead, their shadows flickering across the forest floor. It was a reminder that the jungle still held many secrets, some of them beyond their understanding.

As the pterosaurs moved on, the group continued their journey, the encounter adding a new layer of wonder and caution to their expedition. The forest seemed even more alive now, every rustle in the underbrush, every call from the treetops, a potential harbinger of the unknown.

That evening, they set up camp in a clearing, the sounds of the forest a comforting backdrop to their activities. As they prepared dinner, Miguel approached the group, a triumphant grin on his face. In his hands, he held a large, pale egg.

"Found this in a pterosaur nest," he announced, holding it up for everyone to see. "Thought it might make a good addition to our meal."

"You are either brave or stupid, Miguel," responded Juan. Everyone smiled at the words.

Carl followed up in serious tone. "Goodness, we must assume the former!"

The egg was carefully cracked open, and its contents were added to their stew. As they ate, the taste of the pterosaur egg mingled with the flavors of the jungle, a unique and exotic experience that none of them would soon forget.

Around the campfire, the mood was one of quiet reflection and camaraderie. They spoke of their journey, of the dangers they had faced and the wonders they had seen. The loss of Luis was still fresh in their minds, but the beauty of the Guanacaste region and the marvels they encountered helped to ease the pain.

As the firelight flickered and the jungle sounds lulled them into a sense of peace, Karl looked at his companions, feeling a deep sense of connection and gratitude. They were on an extraordinary journey, one that would test their limits and expand their horizons. And with the mighty Arenal behind them and the enigmatic Tamacún ahead, their adventure was far from over.

Tamacún

DAYS HAD TURNED INTO weeks since they left Puerto Limón, the landscape gradually changing as they ascended the slopes of Rincón de la Vieja. The air grew cooler, and the vegetation became sparser, giving way to rocky outcrops and steaming vents. The journey tested their endurance, but Karl was driven by an insatiable curiosity and a desire to uncover the secrets of the volcano.

One afternoon, as they neared their destination, a sudden rumble shook the ground beneath their feet. Karl looked up to see a plume of smoke rising from the crater of Rincón de la Vieja. The volcano was awake, a reminder of the raw power that lay beneath the surface. It was also an unfortunate reminder of their colleague, Luis.

"We're close," Manuel said, his voice tinged with awe. "Be ready for anything."

Karl nodded, feeling a mix of excitement and trepidation. The adventure had brought them to the very edge of the world, where the earth itself seemed to breathe with a fiery spirit. He knew that the journey was far from over and that the true test of their resolve was yet to come. Carl, however, was terrified of the whole thing. This was more than he had anticipated, and he wanted no part of it. But nonetheless, he stayed close to the others.

As they approached the summit, Karl could feel the heat radiating from the ground. The air was thick with the scent of sulfur, and the landscape was marked by fumaroles and boiling mudpits, the very lifeblood of the volcano seeping to the surface. Manuel and the others moved with a cautious respect, aware that one misstep could lead to disaster.

Karl set up his equipment, eager to begin his observations. He marveled at the sheer force of nature before him, the ground rumbling beneath his feet as if alive with an ancient, primordial energy. As he sketched the landscape and took measurements, a sense of awe and humility filled him. Here, in the presence of such raw power, he felt a deep connection to the earth and its mysteries.

But the journey was not without its challenges. One night, as they camped near a fumarole, a sudden eruption startled them awake. A jet of steam and ash shot into the air, and the ground trembled violently. Karl and his team scrambled to safety, their hearts pounding with fear.

"Is everyone all right?" Karl called out, his voice barely audible over the roar of the eruption.

One by one, his companions emerged from the darkness, shaken but unharmed. Manuel's face was set in a grim expression.

"We need to move to a safer location," he said. "The volcano is unpredictable. We cannot take any chances."

They packed up their camp and moved further down the slope, finding a more secure spot to set up their tents. The rest of the night was tense, the threat of another eruption hanging over them like a dark cloud. Chico was nowhere to be found.

Despite the dangers, Karl's determination never wavered. He was here to document the volcano, to understand its behavior and contribute to the growing body of geological knowledge. Each day brought new discoveries—mineral deposits, unique rock formations, and the ever-present steam vents that hissed and sputtered like living creatures.

As they continued their observations, Karl couldn't help but think of the legends Manuel had mentioned. The spirits of the jungle, the ancient guardians—perhaps there was some truth to the stories. In this wild and untamed land, the line between myth and reality seemed to blur.

Eager to get back to birding, Carl had asked if he could head down the volcano and do more study of the local birds from there. It was simply too dangerous to go alone and all of the company were needed here in case camp needed to be moved again, or worse: someone needed medical attention from the unpredictable.

One evening, as they sat around the campfire, Juan shared a story passed down from his ancestors. He spoke of a great warrior who had once climbed the volcano to seek wisdom from the gods. According to the legend, the warrior had encountered spirits who tested his courage and resolve, ultimately granting him the knowledge he sought.

Karl listened intently, the flickering flames casting eerie shadows on the faces of his companions. The story resonated with him, a reminder that the journey was not just a physical challenge, but a spiritual one as well.

For several days, they explored the slopes of Rincón de la Vieja, each step bringing them closer to understanding the volcano's secrets. Karl's journals filled with notes and sketches, a testament to their relentless pursuit of knowledge.

As they prepared to leave the volcano and return to Puerto Limón, Karl felt a profound sense of accomplishment. The journey had tested their limits, pushing them to the brink and back. But it had also revealed the beauty and majesty of the natural world, a reminder of the delicate balance between humanity and the forces of nature.

With Manuel and his team by his side, Karl knew that they had forged a bond that would last a lifetime. They had faced the unknown together, emerging stronger and wiser for it. As they made their way back through the jungle, the spirits of the forest seemed to whisper their approval, a silent acknowledgment of the journey they had undertaken.

The adventure was far from over. Karl's heart was already filled with plans for future expeditions, new horizons to explore, and more mysteries to unravel. But for now, he savored the triumph of their journey to Tamacún, the volcano that had tested their mettle and revealed the enduring spirit of discovery.

The Haunting of Tamacún

IN THE DISTANCE, THE source of this expedition could still be seen, its tall summit rising above everything around it. Karl had achieved his primary objective, and now they were headed back the same way they had come. Journals were full of detailed information and data that would help him and many others better understand these unpredictable monsters. From Pompeii to Luis' death at Arenal, it was vital more warning signs could be used to announce an eruption before it started. Lives could be saved. It was as simple as that.

As the group made their way through the dense foliage of the jungle, the atmosphere seemed to change. The air grew thicker, the shadows deeper. It was as if the very forest was closing in around them, whispering secrets from ages past. Karl couldn't shake the feeling that they were being watched, not by the eyes of curious animals, but by something more sinister, more ancient.

One evening, as they set up camp near a small clearing, the feeling of unease intensified. The usual sounds of the jungle—chirping insects, distant calls of nocturnal creatures—were eerily absent. An unnatural silence enveloped the camp, broken only by the crackling of their fire. Manuel, usually stoic and unflappable, seemed tense, his eyes darting nervously to the shadows beyond the firelight.

As darkness fell, the unease turned to palpable fear. Strange shapes flitted at the edges of their vision, and whispers, almost human but not quite, drifted through the air. Carl, usually rational and composed, looked shaken. "Karl, do you feel that? It's like we're not alone here," he said, his voice barely above a whisper.

Manuel nodded grimly. "The spirits of Tamacún," he said, his voice low. "Ancient guardians of this land. They do not like intruders."

The firelight cast long shadows that seemed to move of their own accord. The jungle around them felt alive with unseen eyes. Then, without warning, the temperature dropped, a cold chill sweeping through the camp. The fire flickered and almost went out, as if an unseen hand was trying to snuff it out.

It was Juan who first saw them. "Look!" he shouted, pointing to the edge of the clearing. There, just beyond the light of the fire, were ghostly apparitions. They were vaguely human in shape but translucent, with hollow eyes that seemed to stare into their very souls.

The camp erupted in chaos. Chico, Manuel's coatimundi, chittered nervously, darting back and forth. The men grabbed whatever they could use as weapons—knives, sticks, even stones—and formed a tight circle around the fire.

The ghosts did not move closer, but their presence was suffocating. Karl felt a cold hand on his shoulder and turned, but there was nothing there. The whispers grew louder, a cacophony of unintelligible words, and the shadows seemed to press in tighter.

"We *must* do something," Carl said, his voice trembling. "We can't just stand here and wait for them to... to do whatever it is they're planning."

Manuel stepped forward, his face set in determination. "We must drive them away," he said. "These spirits are tied to this land, but they fear fire and the strength of the living."

With Manuel leading the way, the group began to chant, their voices rising above the whispers of the spirits. They brandished their makeshift weapons, swinging them through the air as if to cut through the shadows themselves. The fire, once flickering and weak, seemed to grow stronger, its light pushing back the darkness.

The spirits recoiled, their forms flickering and becoming less distinct. The temperature began to rise again, the oppressive cold lifting. But the spirits did not leave easily. They howled in anger, a sound that pierced through the night and sent chills down the spines of the men.

One of the ghosts rushed forward towards Carl who simply held up his hands in defense. "Go away!" he exclaimed as it neared him.

"En el nombre de Dios y por la sangre de Cristo, te ordeno que te vayas." That came from Juan who moved quickly to stand between Carl and the apparition. His words matched the hard look on his face, and he held his torch of fire in front of him.

The ghost, seemingly taken aback by his words, retreated to its companions, hissing and other undiscernible noises coming from it as it did.

Finally, with one last surge of energy, the spirits dissipated, melting back into the shadows of the jungle. The fire roared, casting a warm, protective glow over the camp. The whispers ceased, and the normal sounds of the jungle slowly returned.

The men stood in stunned silence, their hearts pounding in their chests. They had driven the spirits away, but the encounter had left them shaken and exhausted. It was clear that this place, Tamacún, was not just a volcano but a land steeped in ancient power and mystery.

"We can't stay here," Karl said, his voice hoarse. "We need to keep moving. It's not safe."

Manuel nodded in agreement. "Yes, we must leave this place. The spirits may return, and next time, we may not be so fortunate."

They quickly packed up their camp, their movements hurried and tense. The jungle, once a place of danger but also of beauty, now felt hostile and alien. They moved through the night, guided by Manuel and Miguel, who knew the jungle paths well.

As they walked, Karl couldn't help but think about the spirits they had encountered. Who were they? Guardians of the land, as Manuel had said? Or something more? The questions swirled in his mind, but he knew there would be no answers tonight.

They wandered along the paths as best they could in the dark, focused more on distance than staying on the known paths. Dangers existed in the jungle night, and it was not uncommon to come upon a jaguar on the hunt. Shadows still appeared at the edges of their minds, making it difficult to focus on their return path paired with any hazards that ley ahead of them.

As they pressed forward, Karl's senses seemed to heighten, every rustle of leaves or snap of a twig sending shivers down his spine. The jungle at night was a cacophony of unseen movements, a symphony of hidden dangers. He kept his grip tight on the machete, his knuckles white with tension.

Manuel walked ahead, his steps sure and confident, as if he knew exactly where they were headed despite the darkness obscuring their surroundings. Karl marveled at his guide's resilience, his unwavering determination in the face of uncertainty. It was as if Manuel had a sixth sense guiding him through the labyrinthine paths of the jungle.

Suddenly, a low growl shattered the silence, freezing the party in their tracks. Carl felt the hairs on the back of his neck stand on end as he strained to locate the source of the sound. Manuel turned back, his expression grim.

"Jaguar," he whispered, his voice barely audible over the pounding of Carl's heart. "We need to move, but cautiously. They're most active at night."

With every step they took, the darkness seemed to close in around them, swallowing them whole. Karl couldn't shake the feeling that they were being watched, that unseen eyes were tracking their every move. He gripped the machete tighter, his palms slick with sweat.

But despite the fear gnawing at his insides, everyone pressed on, their determination fueled by the hope of reaching safety before the night was over. For they knew that in the heart of the jungle, where shadows danced and spirits roamed, only the strongest would survive.

The Journey Back to Puerto Limón

BY DAWN, THEY HAD PUT a considerable distance between themselves and Tamacún. Exhausted but relieved, they found a small clearing and set up a temporary camp. They were far from safe, but at least, for now, they had escaped the spirits of Tamacún.

Sitting around the fire, their faces illuminated by its warm glow, they shared a silent meal. The encounter had left them all changed, their bond strengthened by the shared experience of facing the unknown. They knew that their journey was far from over, and that many more challenges lay ahead. But for now, they were together, and that was enough.

As they discussed their next steps, Manuel suggested a route that would take them north of Arenal. "We need to decide on our route back to Puerto Limón," he said, his voice steady but tinged with concern. "Heading north of Arenal might be our safest option, but we must be cautious."

Karl nodded, still haunted by the earlier events but determined to lead his team to safety. "What lies to the north, Manuel? Are there any known dangers or obstacles?"

Manuel scratched his chin thoughtfully. "The terrain is rough, mostly dense jungle. There are no known settlements, which could be both a blessing and a curse. Fewer people means fewer threats, but also less help if we need it."

Juan, who had been silent, added, "I can set up camp anywhere, but the jungle can be treacherous. We should avoid any unnecessary risks. What about water sources?"

Miguel, ever the tracker, spoke next. "There are streams and rivers that flow from Arenal. If we follow them, we can find fresh water and navigate more easily. It's a natural guide."

Manuel nodded, his confidence growing with each question. "Yes, the northern route has plenty of resources. It's challenging, but together, we can make it."

Karl looked around at his team, their faces illuminated by the fire. Despite their exhaustion and the fear that still lingered, he saw determination and trust. "North it is, then," he said firmly. "We'll face whatever comes our way together." With a unanimous decision, they resolved to make the journey northward, eager to uncover the secrets that awaited them.

Manuel smiled, feeling a sense of unity among the group. "We leave en la mañana. Rest now, my friends. We have a long journey ahead."

With that, the company settled in for the night, their thoughts already turning to the challenges and adventures that lay before them on the path north of Arenal.

The following days were filled with treacherous terrain and dense foliage, but the promise of discovery kept them moving forward. Miguel, with his keen tracking skills, led the way, his eyes trained on the slightest signs of a path through the wilderness.

As they journeyed north of Arenal, the group moved cautiously, guided by Manuel's knowledge of the terrain and Miguel's sharp tracking skills. The jungle was dense and unforgiving, but they pressed on, driven by a mixture of curiosity and necessity.

One late afternoon, as the light began to dim and the forest shadows lengthened, Miguel halted abruptly. "There's something here," he called back to the group, his voice echoing slightly in the still air.

The company gathered around, peering into the thick underbrush. Manuel pushed forward, parting the foliage with his machete. "It looks like an opening," he said, his voice filled with intrigue. "A cave, perhaps."

Karl, always the scientist, stepped closer, examining the dark entrance. "We should explore it. Caves can tell us a lot about the geological activity in this region, and we might find shelter for the night."

Carl nodded, his ornithological interests piqued by the possibility of discovering cave-dwelling birds. "Let's see what's inside. We have enough supplies to venture in for a short time."

Juan and Manuel exchanged glances, the practical men of the group. "We should be cautious," Juan warned. "Caves can be dangerous, especially if we're not prepared."

Manuel agreed but was already pulling out a lantern. "We'll proceed carefully. Everyone stay close and watch your step."

With a mix of excitement and apprehension, they entered the cave. The air inside was cool and damp, a stark contrast to the humid jungle outside. The flickering light from their lanterns cast eerie shadows on the walls, revealing ancient stalactites and stalagmites.

As they ventured deeper, the cave opened into a series of chambers, each more magnificent than the last. The ceilings were high, adorned with natural formations that sparkled in the lantern light. The sound of dripping water echoed through the space, creating an almost mystical atmosphere.

"This place is incredible," Karl whispered, his voice full of awe. "It's like stepping into another world."

Carl agreed, his eyes wide with wonder. "Who knows what we might find here? This could be a significant discovery."

Manuel led the way, his experienced eyes scanning the cave for any signs of danger. "Let's explore a bit more, but we mustn't lose track of time. We need to find a safe place to rest for the night."

The group continued their exploration, each step revealing more of the cave's secrets. The animals discovered them long before the humans were aware they had company. Running through the group of men were a group of five deer. Three does and two fawn sprinted past the company, headed outwards through the cave's entrance.

"Venado," Miguel offered. "Deer, señores."

Stepping into the darkness, they were enveloped by an eerie silence broken only by the sound of their footsteps echoing off the walls. The air grew thick and musty, making it difficult to breathe as they descended deeper into the labyrinth.

But as they pressed forward, their excitement turned to apprehension as they realized they had lost their sense of direction. Panic began to set in as they realized they were trapped within the maze of tunnels, their only source of light fading with each passing moment.

"We must find a way out," Karl urged, his voice tinged with desperation. "Before it's too late."

But as they searched for an escape route, their torches flickered and died, leaving them stranded in the darkness. The air grew thin, suffocating them as they struggled to find a way to the surface.

Just when all hope seemed lost, Carl spotted a bat fluttering above them, its wings brushing against the rocky ceiling. With a swift motion, he shooed the creature away, following its erratic flight path through the maze of tunnels.

"It's our only chance," he declared, his voice echoing off the walls as they followed the bat into the unknown.

With renewed determination, they pressed forward, their hearts pounding in their chests as they chased after the elusive creature. And finally, after what felt like an eternity, they emerged into the blinding light of day, their lungs gasping for air as they collapsed onto the forest floor.

They lay there for a moment, catching their breath as they basked in the warmth of the sun. They had survived the ordeal, their bond stronger than ever as they faced yet another challenge together.

"I will call them," Manuel said, struggling to catch his breath, "Cavernas de Venado." And so the name stuck until this day.

But as they made their way back to Puerto Limón, their minds were filled with thoughts of the journey that lay ahead. And with each passing moment, they grew more determined to uncover the mysteries that awaited them in the wilds of Costa Rica.

The Port City of Puerto Limón

IT WAS ANOTHER WEEK before they reached Puerto Limón, but it had been without further adventure. Karl found himself almost bored with the trek back to the port city, but Carl had found his time filled with new ornithological discoveries, and his journal filled as a result. The former had taken the extra time to draft a rough sketch of a map of the area, the earlier parts of it from memories of their adventures. Both East and West coasts of Costa Rica were well-known, but he was able to fill in gaps for much of the interior of the country.

Carl was certain he had uncovered several new bird species which would be of great interest to his colleagues and friends back in Hamburg and elsewhere in Europe. From colorful parrots to tropical quetzals, he had detailed records and several drawings, although he would need to fill in the color back home. He had even collected a few specimens for further study.

As they descended from the highlands and made their way towards Puerto Limón, the landscape gradually shifted. The dense jungles gave way to sprawling banana plantations, and the air grew thick with the scent of salt and the promise of the sea. Karl and his companions felt a mix of relief and anticipation as the bustling port city came into view.

Puerto Limón, founded in 1854, had quickly risen to prominence due to its strategic location on the Caribbean coast. It served as a crucial gateway for Costa Rica's trade, facilitating the export of coffee and bananas to Europe and North America. The city's growth had been fueled by the construction of the railroad, which connected it to the capital, San José, and allowed for the efficient transportation of goods.

The city itself was a vibrant mosaic of cultures, with a diverse population that included indigenous people, Afro-Caribbean descendants, and immigrants from Europe and Asia. The streets were lined with colorful buildings, their facades weathered by the tropical climate. The harbor was a hive of activity, with ships from around the world docked alongside local fishing boats.

Karl marveled at the bustling marketplace, where merchants hawked their wares, from exotic fruits and spices to handmade crafts. The air was filled with the sounds of haggling and the clatter of goods being unloaded. He could see that Puerto Limón was not just a port but a thriving community, a vital artery in the economic lifeblood of Costa Rica.

As they made their way through the crowded streets, Manuel guided them to a warehouse where they would offload their supplies. Juan and Miguel immediately set to work, their strong backs and practiced hands making quick work of the heavy crates and equipment. Karl took a moment to appreciate the significance of their journey, knowing that their discoveries and experiences would contribute to the greater understanding of this rich and diverse land.

Carl, meanwhile, was already deep in conversation with a local merchant, excitedly sharing his ornithological findings. He had arranged for his specimens and notes to be shipped back to Europe, eager to share his discoveries with the scientific community. His enthusiasm was infectious, and Karl couldn't help but smile at his friend's boundless energy.

The unloading process took the better part of the afternoon, and as the sun began to set, the team gathered one last time by the docks. They had survived the perils of the jungle, faced the supernatural, and emerged stronger for it. Their bond, forged in the crucible of adventure, was unbreakable.

"We've come a long way," Karl said, his voice filled with gratitude and a touch of nostalgia. "And for now, our journey is over. This would not have been possible without each one of you."

Manuel nodded, his eyes reflecting the wisdom of someone who had spent a lifetime exploring the wilds of Costa Rica. "Indeed, señor. The jungle is vast and full of secrets. But for now, we rest."

With that, they parted ways, each man heading off to attend to his own tasks. Karl and Carl would prepare for their return to Europe, their minds already buzzing with plans for future expeditions. Manuel, Juan, and Miguel would remain in Puerto Limón, their skills and knowledge invaluable to any who sought to explore the untamed heart of Costa Rica.

As the stars began to twinkle in the night sky, the city of Puerto Limón settled into a peaceful rhythm. The adventure had ended, but the legacy of their journey would live on, etched in the annals of history and the memories of those who dared to explore the unknown.

Farewells and Goodbyes

AFTER SO MANY WEEKS in the jungle, the sounds of the city seemed odd to Karl. Sleeping in a bed was somewhat uncomfortable; he tossed a lot in an attempt to release the day to his dreams.

Carl took notice. "Travel to foreign places always leaves us with things we cannot take with us, nor leave behind."

"But this one will linger for longer than the others, "replied Karl. Eventually sleep would overtake his conscious mind, but for the time being, he could only think of spirits, jaguars, and creatures he thought had died out a long time ago.

· · · ·

The morning came too soon, the sun's rays piercing through the thin curtains of their modest lodging. The day ahead was filled with farewells and preparations for their departure. As they gathered their belongings, a heavy sense of finality hung in the air. The jungle, with its mysteries and dangers, had forged a bond between them that would be difficult to sever.

They met Manuel, Juan, and Miguel at the docks, where their ship awaited to take them to Havana and ultimately back to Hamburg. The farewells were heartfelt, each man expressing gratitude and respect for the others. Manuel, always stoic, allowed a rare smile to break across his face as he shook Karl's hand.

"You are always welcome in Costa Rica, my friend," he said. "May your journey be safe and your discoveries plentiful."

"Thank you, Manuel," Karl replied, his voice thick with emotion. "We owe our lives to you. I hope we meet again someday."

Juan and Miguel added their goodbyes, each with a firm handshake and a promise to stay in touch. Karl turned to Chico, the little coatimundi that had become a symbol of their adventure. He crouched down, scratching the animal behind the ears.

"Take care of Manuel, Chico," he said softly. Chico chirped in response, nuzzling Karl's hand before scampering back to Manuel.

With their farewells said, Karl and Carl boarded the ship, their hearts heavy but their spirits high. The ship's horn blared as it pulled away from the dock, the city of Puerto Limón gradually shrinking into the distance. The journey home would be long, but they were eager to return there and share their findings with the world.

The days at sea were spent organizing their notes and specimens. Carl meticulously reviewed his ornithological discoveries, his journal pages filled with sketches and descriptions of the birds they had encountered. Karl worked on his maps and observations, ensuring that every detail of their journey was recorded.

"We've seen so much," Carl remarked one evening as they sat on the deck, the sun setting over the horizon. "It's hard to believe it's all real."

"Indeed," Karl replied. "Costa Rica is a land of wonders. The beauty and danger coexist in a way that is both humbling and inspiring."

As they neared Havana, their anticipation grew. The Cuban capital would be a brief stop before their final leg to Europe, and they looked forward to the chance to rest and resupply. The bustling port of Havana was a stark contrast to the wilds of Costa Rica, yet it carried its own charm and vibrancy.

Once in Hamburg, Karl and Carl were greeted with curiosity and excitement by their peers. The scientific community was eager to hear about their adventures and discoveries. Karl's maps and Carl's ornithological records were met with acclaim, and they were soon busy preparing their journals for publication.

In the quiet moments, however, Karl found himself reminiscing about Costa Rica. The memories of their journey through the dense jungles, the eerie encounters with spirits, and the breathtaking views from the peaks of Tamacún were etched into his mind. He knew that no matter how many adventures he undertook, Costa Rica would always hold a special place in his heart.

As he sat at his desk, putting the final touches on his journal, Karl reflected on the profound impact the journey had on him. The country had revealed its wonders to him in ways he could never have imagined. From the vibrant wildlife to the rich cultural heritage, Costa Rica was a land of endless discovery.

Its rainforests, teeming with life, were a testament to the raw beauty of nature. The volcanoes, with their formidable presence, spoke of the earth's incredible power. The people, resilient and welcoming, showcased a spirit that was as vibrant as the land itself.

Karl knew that their published works would bring attention to Costa Rica, highlighting its importance both scientifically and culturally. But he also knew that the true essence of the country could only be experienced firsthand. He hoped that others would be inspired to explore its depths, to uncover its secrets, and to appreciate its splendor.

As he sealed the last envelope, ready to send off his findings to the publishers, Karl felt a sense of fulfillment. Their journey had been perilous and challenging, but it had also been profoundly rewarding. Costa Rica had given them more than they could ever have imagined, and in return, they had captured its essence to share with the world.

With a deep breath, Karl stood and gazed out the window at the bustling streets of Hamburg. The world was vast, filled with countless wonders waiting to be discovered. But no matter where his future adventures took him, a part of his heart would always remain in Costa Rica, the land of eternal enchantment.

Don't miss out!

Visit the website below and you can sign up to receive emails whenever David Robertson publishes a new book. There's no charge and no obligation.

https://books2read.com/r/B-A-WMROB-SSDOD

BOOKS 2 READ

Connecting independent readers to independent writers.

About the Author

After starting his career as a programmer with NASA working on the International Space Station, David Robertson moved on to designing and building computer software. He currently works as a software architect.

His struggling career as a musician keeps his focus on architecting software platforms, but he still enjoys playing the guitar whenever he can. Lately, solar and wind systems help entertain his engineer's mind, and give him chances to collaborate on those things with his kids. One day soon, he plans to thru-hike some of the big trails in North America and hopefully Europe.

About the Publisher

Tomorrow's Tales - follow us on Facebook: https://www.facebook.com/profile.php?id=61564844791784

Read more at https://tomorrowstales.beehiiv.com/subscribe.